Be sure to look for all the great McGee and Me! books and videos at your favorite bookstore.

Episode One:
"The Big Lie"
A great adventure in honesty.

Episode Two:
"A Star in the Breaking"
A great adventure in humility.

Episode Three:
"The Not-So-Great Escape"
A great adventure in obedience.

Episode Four:
"Skate Expectations"
A great adventure in kindness.

Episode Five:
"Twister and Shout"
A great adventure in faith.

Focus on the Family®

PRESENTS

Back
to the
Drawing
Board

Bill Myers

Based on characters created by Bill Myers and Ken C. Johnson
and on the teleplay by Janet Scott Batchler and Lee Batchler.

Tyndale House Publishers, Inc.
Wheaton, Illinois

For John M. Dettoni, who laid McGee's foundation

Front cover illustration copyright © 1990 by Morgan Weistling
Interior illustrations by Nathan Greene, copyright © 1990 by
Tyndale House Publishers, Inc.

Library of Congress Catalog Card Number 90-70609
ISBN 0-8423-4111-0
McGee and Me!, McGee, and *McGee and Me!* logo
are trademarks of Living Bibles International
Copyright © 1990 by Living Bibles International
All rights reserved
Printed in the United States of America

Contents

For wherever there is jealousy or selfish ambition, there will be disorder and every other kind of evil (James 3:16, *The Living Bible*).

ONE
The Return of Spam Shade

It was warmer than the back of a TV set after thirty hours of nonstop Nintendo. Hotter than the back of some kid's pants after Mom catches him giving the poodle a trim job with Dad's electric razor. It was so hot and humid I did what any world-famous cartoon character playing a private eye would do . . . I sweated.

I sat and sweated. I sweated and sat. Then, just when I was sure I'd sweated all the sweat a sweet, sentimental slob like me could sweat, I sat and sweated some more.

And then it happened . . . the phone rang.

I picked it up and answered. "Spam Shade—Private Guy."

It was the wife of our beloved president—the first lady herself, Barbara Brush. Barbie (as her friends call her) and her husband Ken had been good buddies of mine ever since I first met them in Jamie's toy chest. In fact, I had even dated Barbie's younger sister, Skipper, once or twice.

Now the family needed my help.

"Spam," she pleaded. "You're our last hope! This horrific hot weather is the work of that truly terrible, tyrannical tyrant—"

"You don't mean . . . ," I interrupted.

"Yes," she gasped. "That tawny, troublesome, traitor . . . Tan Man!"

Suddenly there was a blast of scary music. (That always happens when the bad guy is mentioned in these cheap detective fantasies. But that's OK, by now I was used to it.) Then there was a loud crackle on the phone as if someone had just tapped into my line, and I heard another voice. . . .

"Hey, like wow, dude. Isn't this weather totally excellent?"

A cold shudder shuddered through me. It was Tan Man. I could tell by the California accent and the fifteen-word vocabulary.

"Tan Man!" I shouted. "So you're behind all this heat."

He gave a laugh that could only come from somebody with blond hair, blue eyes, and an incredibly bronzed body. "What a righteous guess, dude. I've, like, frozen all of the world's thermostats at ninety-six degrees. They're, ya know, heating up the atmosphere so we'll never have winter again. It's just gonna be, like, sun and surf and sand forever and ever."

"But it's the middle of December." I tried to reason with him.

"Yeah, well, looks like Santa's going to have to get some righteous Bermudas and trade his sleigh in for a board, dude."

"But . . ."

He cut me off with another one of his mindless California laughs (is there any other kind of California laugh?) and hung up.

"Did you get all of that?" It was Barbara, still on the other end. "Our government has tried everything we know and we still can't find him. Can you help?"

"No sweat," I said. (An obvious lie, since I was wiping another half gallon of perspiration off my forehead.)

"The fate of the entire world rests on your shoulders, Spam."

"So what else is new?" I said in my ever-so-humble way. "Just relax, Barbie. I'm on my way!"

I hung up and raced outside to my car. The street was a jungle . . . literally. It had been so hot for so long that palm plants, banana trees, and vines had grown everywhere. I grabbed the safari hat and machete I keep in the glove compartment for just such occasions and started off on foot.

Crocodiles were snapping and snarling from every puddle and ditch. Obviously they hoped my delectable tootsies would come in range for a little between-meal snack. But since we cartoon types only have eight toes to begin with, I figured this was no time to be generous and stop to feed the animals.

Suddenly there was an ear-splitting roar. I spun around just in time to see a lion with teeth the size of Toledo leaping at me. I threw my ever-nimble body to the ground and expertly rolled out of the way—and just in time! Ol' Leo definitely thought I was his next bowl of Little Friskies.

Well, I was not afraid. How could I be? I'm the hero in this story. Besides, I know how to deal with lions—I've been to the circus. I quickly grabbed a chair and whip (which I also keep handy for such occasions) and lit a nearby Hula-Hoop. Now, if I could just get ol' Puss 'n Boots here to jump through that hoop, maybe sit up on his hind legs and wave to the crowd . . .

I snapped the whip and stuck out the chair, which he immediately grabbed and chomped to bits. Hey, I wasn't worried. I figured the ol' fur face just needed more fiber in his diet. Then he grabbed the whip and started to floss his fangs with it, and I realized we obviously hadn't been to the same circus. I mean, no way was I going to stick my head in his mouth for the grand finale. He was just going to have to find another dessert. No hot fudge McGees for him.

I had no choice: it was time to use my secret weapon. A weapon only we highly trained and best-dressed detectives can use . . . a weapon so powerful we use it only as a last resort . . . a weapon you kids at home should never try on your own—I reached into my back pocket and pulled out a saucer of milk.

Immediately, Mr. King of the Jungle began to purr and rub against my leg.

"Take it easy, boy," I giggled. "Easy, big fella. . . ."

But my victory was short-lived. Immediately, an arm hairier than any football coach's grabbed me by the neck and pulled me into a nearby tree. One of the gorillas had mistaken my yellow hair for a banana, and now she was doing her best to try to peel me!

"Me no banana!" I shouted in my best gorilla-ese. "Me McGee!"

It did no good. I mean, with all of her squeezing and pulling and poking I was about to split a gut . . . literally. In a last-ditch effort I reached into my shirt and pulled out my handy-dandy gorilla mask. It did the trick. She took one look at me and immediately fell in love. (How could she do otherwise?)

Then things started to get out of hand. This she-gorilla really started going ape over me. I mean, talk about having a crush on someone. She held me so tight I could barely breathe as we started swinging from vine to vine.

"Come on, honey!" I shouted between muffled gasps. "Let's stop monkeying around."

Unfortunately, she had no sense of humor. Instead, she dropped to the jungle floor, tucked me under her arm like a football, and made for the goal line—her house. She must have been in a hurry to introduce me to Mom and Dad. Shoot, I hadn't even popped the question yet!

Things were looking bad. It's not that she wasn't sweet. She had a fine personality, I could get use to the banana breath, and I'd never have to worry about buying her a fur coat. But, hey, let's face it, she just wasn't the "Gorill-a my Dreams." (Was that a groan I heard?)

I didn't see any way out. So I did what any smart cartoon character would do: I started crying for the artist. "Nicholas! Get me out of this! Nicholas . . . !!"

Suddenly a huge #2 pencil appeared out of nowhere. Of course it belonged to my good buddy and creator, Nicholas Martin. As I watched (from under a furry arm) he quickly sketched a giant banana peel right in front of Miss Kong's furry feet. It did the trick! She stepped on the peel and went sliding out of the picture faster than you can say "Chiquita Banana."

I, on the other hand, was thrown into the air. When I came down, I landed right in the middle of . . . Tan Man's camp! What luck! Quickly I looked around. The smell of coconut butter and Sunscreen #7 was suffocating, and all around me were Tan Man's "Raisinettes" . . . once beautiful babes who'd turned into a mass of wrinkles from all the sun.

Tan Man, on the other hand, was nowhere to be found.

Then I heard him. His voice was muffled and a little put-out. "Nice of you to, like, drop in, dude."

He was underneath me. What luck! I had landed right on top of the sinister surfer. Before I could jump up and scamper to the nearby control panel to reset all of the world's thermostats, Tan Man grabbed me.

I had no choice. I hated to do what I had to do, but I knew I had to do it. I reached down and deftly peeled off my shirt.

Everyone gasped. Some of them dropped to the ground coughing and gagging. Others backed away in horror. My glaring, white body, which had never seen a ray of sun, was more than they could handle.

"No, please, put it back on. . . ." Tan Man whimpered as he tried to cover his eyes from my blinding

white torso. "I can't stand it . . . please . . . please!" He dropped to his knees, sobbing like some kid who'd just found out he had to go to summer school.

I raced to the control panel and with one swift kick knocked the on/off switch to kingdom come. Immediately, things started to cool down. Clouds quickly gathered overhead. It started to blow and rain and freeze.

Ah, victory. . . .

No longer would we be subjected to 365 days of summer. No longer would we go to the beach every day. No longer could we swim any time we wanted. No longer could we . . . hey, wait a minute! What have I done!?

I dropped to my knees and frantically searched for the on/off switch. Maybe we could use a little chewing gum and twine to fix it up again. No such luck. It was too late. The switch had disappeared into the blinding snow storm that had suddenly engulfed us.

Well, what can I say? I had successfully completed another job. The entire free world was once again a safer, if not chillier, place. All because of the genius, super-good looks, creativity, and humility (did I mention super-good looks?) of . . . Spam Shade, Private Guy.

TWO
The New Kid

McGee was enjoying his adventure as Spam Shade almost as much as Nick was enjoying drawing it. Nicholas never knew how his McGee stories would turn out. He'd just sit down, start drawing, and wait to see what happened. Like today's adventure, for example. All he'd known about it was that he wanted a little visit from Tan Man. Maybe it was because he hadn't seen the sun for the last couple of weeks (which probably had something to do with them being smack dab in the middle of winter).

It seemed as though it had been snowing off and on in Eastfield forever. Try as it might, the thermometer just couldn't push itself above freezing. If that wasn't bad enough, a blizzard had hit the night before. It had dumped nearly six inches of snow all over the roads and highways. *All right!* Nick and his friends had thought. *School will be canceled!!*

Of course, they were wrong. For some reason,

the officials seemed determined to keep the schools open. Nick wasn't sure why, but he figured it had something to do with the teachers. They'd probably go through withdrawal if they couldn't give out homework.

So here he sat in Mrs. Harmon's room with the rest of the kids. Mrs. Harmon was a little late this morning, so Nick passed the time by drawing McGee's Spam Shade adventure. He also passed the time by showing off—just a little.

Oh, he didn't start out showing off. He started out drawing. But it wasn't too long before Louis spotted him, and once Louis finds out something, it isn't too long before the whole world finds out. I mean, hey, forget the newspapers, TV, and radio. You don't even need to decide between MCI or AT&T. If you want the world to know something, all you have to do is tell Louis.

"That's great, man!" he exclaimed. "Hey, everybody come over and look at this!"

Before Nicholas knew it, everyone was gathered around his desk watching him draw. They "oooh'd" as he drew McGee leaping over the crocodiles. They "ahh'd" as the little guy fought off the lovesick ape. They laughed and cheered as he crashed on top of Tan Man.

And Nicholas? Well, Nicholas was in heaven. If there was one thing he enjoyed as much as drawing, it was being liked—and being liked was definitely happening this morning.

It hadn't always been that way . . . Nick being liked. As you may recall, when Nick first moved to Eastfield he was anything but liked. That's why he invented the story about the scary Indian and the mysterious house. It was a great story—one that made everyone love him . . . for about three days. Then they found out he was lying, and then he was about as popular as a take-home test over Christmas vacation.

All that was behind him now. Now he was fitting in. Now everyone liked him.

"Yo, what's up, dog face?"

Well, OK, almost everyone. He had never quite worked his way into Derrick Cryder's heart. But that was OK. No one had ever proven Derrick Cryder *had* a heart. All he had was a mouth. A big mouth. Oh yeah, and muscles. Big muscles. Lots and lots of big muscles. Especially in his arms and hands, right where a guy like him needed them so he could pick on other kids.

No one was sure where Derrick Cryder got his size. Maybe it was from all the vitamins he took. Or from all the weights he lifted with his middle school friends. Or maybe it was just because this was the third year in a row he was taking fifth grade!

It didn't matter where he got his size. The point is, you didn't want to get in the way of that size. Especially if he knew you had some extra money in your pocket. Or if he knew you had the answers to last night's homework assignment.

Yes sir, everyone was afraid of Derrick Cryder.

Everyone, that is, but Renee. Somehow she was always able to get away with nailing him with a well-placed zinger. Maybe it was because she was a girl. Or maybe it was because he had a secret crush on her. Most likely, though, it was because she had a secret weapon he didn't have. She had a brain.

"So what are you doing, Martin?" Derrick demanded. "Playing with crayons?"

Everyone grew silent. Everyone but Renee. "Why, Derrick? Are you missing yours?"

The kids snickered.

Derrick glared.

Renee did what she did best. She ignored him. If there's one thing Derrick Cryder hates, it's being ignored. So to prove he was still in charge, he yanked the sketch pad out of Nick's hand and looked at the sketch. It made no sense to Derrick— he couldn't even make out the characters. That is, until Renee took the pad and gently turned it right side up.

More snickering from the kids.

Derrick was fuming. You could almost see the smoke coming out of his ears. It wasn't fair. A bully makes one little mistake, and he starts losing everyone's respect? He tossed the pad back at Nick with his best shot—the ever-so-glib line, "Yeah, well, takes one to know one."

Of course, the line made no sense at all. But no one bothered to tell Derrick that. When you're five-foot-seven in a class of five-footers you can say just about whatever you want, whether it makes sense or not.

Suddenly, Mrs. Harmon appeared in the doorway. Everyone did the usual sprint back to his seat.

"Class, class . . . settle down now."

Beside her stood a kid Nicholas had never seen before. He was an average-looking kid. Average height, average hair, average build.

"I want you all to welcome Todd Burton," Mrs. Harmon continued. "He's just moved to Eastfield."

Suddenly Nick noticed one thing that was not average about Todd. There, under Todd's arm, with the notebook, the text books, and sack lunch . . . with all of that other stuff . . . there was a *sketch pad!*

"We'll spend some time getting to know Todd better before lunch today," Mrs. Harmon said as she directed him to an empty seat across the aisle from Nick's seat. "But first, there's the matter of a little history quiz we need to take."

The kids let out the usual groans and sighs. After all, when you're a fifth grader, you're expected to groan and sigh over a test. It's in your contract. But Nicholas barely heard. His attention was focused on one thing and one thing only: that sketch pad.

"You don't have to take the quiz," she said to Todd. "But could you do something quietly for the next half hour?"

Nicholas continued to stare. For months now he had been the top dog in the drawing department. For months everyone had been oohing and aahhing over his McGees. He had found his niche. He was the classroom artist. Let the others be the brains, the beauties, the jocks, the whatevers. He, Nicholas Martin, was the official cartoon wonder-kid.

But now that was history. Now, suddenly, there

was someone else . . . someone who was moving in on his turf!

The new kid sat down at the desk. "No problem, Mrs. Harmon," Nick heard him say. "I can find something to do." With that, he reached over and pulled out his sketch pad.

Nick stopped breathing. He waited. He watched. Maybe the kid was a hack. Maybe he was just a "wanna-be" artist. If that was the case, Nicholas would be more than happy to share his vast knowledge and experience on the subject. After all, the least he could do was take the kid under his wing and show him the ropes.

Todd quietly tapped the cover of his sketch pad with his fingers.

What are you waiting for!? Nicholas thought. *Would you please hurry up and open it so I can see if you can draw! I mean, hey, I do have a test to take!*

Todd just kept tapping his pad. First one finger, then the other, then the first one again. It was driving Nicholas crazy!

Finally Todd reached for his pencil box.

Mrs. Harmon was passing out the test and giving last-minute instructions. Nick didn't hear a word she said. He didn't hear a thing except the tapping of Todd's fingers and the rattling of his pencil box.

Nick wanted to shout, to scream at the kid to get it over with. He wanted to grab the sketch pad and throw open the cover himself. He didn't, though. He'd have to be able to move to do something like that. And, at the moment, he was frozen.

Then, finally . . . *finally*, Todd took hold of the

cover of the pad and slowly flipped it open. Nick strained to see what was on the page without Todd knowing he was looking. If he could just tilt his head a little . . . that's it . . . just a little more . . .

Finally! Nick had a full view of what was on the page. And what he saw knocked the air right out of his lungs!

I was right in the middle of winning the Wimpyton Tennis Tournament when I heard my little buddy gasp. It made no difference that I was just two strikes from pitching the hockey puck for a no-hitter and running in for the touchdown (we cartoon types have our own rules when it comes to playing tennis . . . or any other sport, for that matter).

The point is, I'd never heard ol' Nicky boy gasp before. I'd heard him cough and choke and cry (usually when older sister Sarah cooked dinner), but I'd never heard him gasp.

So, without a moment's hesitation, I hopped out of my pad and onto his desk. Now I know you're probably wondering how you can hold a tennis tournament inside a sketch pad. I was a little worried about that myself. But you know, once we got the grandstands built and the overhead lighting installed, it wasn't bad.

I threw a glance up at my buddy. He hadn't looked that sick since he tried to watch a whole day of Saturday morning cartoons.

"Hey, Nick!" I called in my ever-cheery voice. "What's up?"

He didn't say a word. He just pointed.

I followed his trembling finger and almost fell off the desk in shock. Across the way there was some new guy with a sketch pad! That wasn't the worst of it, though. There, scrawled across the page, was a magnificent model of mechanical metal that looked like it had just stepped out of the twenty-second century. I mean, this drawing was high-tech to the max. Everything about him was chrome and steel—from his giant steam shovel mouth to his massive robot hands to the single wheel he balanced on and used as a foot.

It was my turn to gasp. "What is it?" I sputtered.

"That's what I want to know," Nick whispered.

We continued to watch as the kid put the final touches on his monstrous metallic masterpiece. Whoever he was, this new guy could draw. No doubt about it.

Finally he finished. Then he wrote in big block letters at the bottom of the page: J-A-W-B-R-E-A-K-E-R.

For a moment, neither Nick nor I said a word. We just kept staring at this stupendous specimen of staggering strength.

"So, uh . . . ," Nick cleared his throat. "What do you think?"

I could tell he was trying to play it cool. Being the great art critic and intellectual genius that I am, I gave it to him straight. "Hmm . . . ah . . . an interesting statement perhaps, but a little too post-neo-modern counter-abstractionist for my tastes."

"What does that mean?!" Nick asked.

He had me there. It was all I could do to say it. Was I supposed to know what it meant, too?

Suddenly Mrs. Harmon appeared and slapped

the history quiz on Nick's desk. It was time for him to get to work. He grabbed a pencil and did his best to concentrate on the test. I could tell my little pal's mind wasn't on history. It was somewhere in the twenty-second century, battling a bothersome bucket of bolts called Jawbreaker.

THREE
Jealousy Grows . . .

Nicholas was definitely having trouble concentrating on the history quiz. It was fill-in-the-blanks. Usually Nick was a great fill-in-the-blanker. This time he just stared at the first blank for almost five minutes—and he still didn't have a clue to the answer.

It didn't take long for Mrs. Harmon to notice. She strolled on over behind Nick and took a look at his paper. Now, she's not in the habit of helping students on tests, but Nicholas was obviously having some sort of brain drain. So, to help get him started, she leaned over and pointed to the first blank.

"Nicholas Martin," she said.

"I'm sorry, what?" Nick's mind snapped back to the present. Mrs. Harmon was leaning over his shoulder and pointing at the first blank.

"Here," she said, "where it says 'Name?' you want to write, 'Nicholas Martin.'"

Nicholas looked up and gave a sheepish little

grin. "Oh, uh, right. Thanks," he said as he quickly scribbled out his name.

Mrs. Harmon gave him a puzzled smile and moved back toward her desk. Something was definitely on that boy's mind, and it sure wasn't history.

Eventually the bell rang for recess. Nick was shocked. It seemed like they had just started the test. Oh well, at least he'd gotten one right answer . . . the part about his name.

He looked around and caught a glimpse of the new kid just as he headed out the door. Quickly Nick took off after him. He worked his way through the crowd and out the door into the hall.

"Todd!" he called, squirming his way past the other kids. "Todd."

At last Todd heard him and came to a stop. Now, Todd wasn't mean or anything like that. He just wasn't overly friendly. He was . . . polite. No more, no less.

"Hi, I'm Nicholas Martin."

Todd looked at him, waiting for more.

"I, uh, I saw you drawing back in class."

"Oh?" Todd said as he glanced at his watch.

Somehow Nick got the impression he was boring the kid.

"So, uh . . . " Nick cleared his throat still trying to sound cheerful. "What were you drawing?"

With one easy move Todd reached for his sketch pad and flipped it open. There he was in all of his glory: "J-A-W-B-R-E-A-K-E-R!"

There was a low, long whistle. Nick looked around. Louis! Nick didn't know how Louis did it, but the guy always seemed to be at the right place at the right time. And the right place right now seemed to be peering over Todd's shoulder at the drawing.

"Cool," Louis chirped. "Does he open up with, like, lasers and blasters and stuff inside?"

Nick could only roll his eyes at Louis's stupidity. No way could any kid draw all that stuff.

"Oh sure," Todd gloated. "He's fully three-dimensional."

OK, so Todd wasn't just "any" kid.

By now others had started to gather around. "That's outstanding!" they exclaimed. "Excellent!"

Nick let out a long sigh. What was with these people? Hadn't they seen cartoon sketches before?

"Awesome! What do you call him?" Everyone was crowding in for a better look.

"I call him 'Jawbreaker.'"

"That's hot. . . . "

Nick could feel the tops of his ears starting to burn. What he wasn't sure about was why. Who was he mad at? Todd? Todd hadn't done anything to him. The kids? It wasn't their fault it took so little to impress them. So what was his problem?

"Nick can draw, too." It was Louis again. Good ol' Louis. Always there to look out for his friend. What a pal. "Show him, Nick."

"Yeah, sure." Nicholas couldn't help breaking into a grin as he flipped open his sketch pad. Let Mr. Macho super-tech artist take a gander at some *real* artwork.

"See," Louis glowed proudly. "That's Nick's drawing. That's McGee."

Good ol' Louis, Nick thought. *What a guy. True*

to the end. Nick turned to see Todd's expression. Hey . . . what was that? Could it be? Was that . . . was that a yawn escaping from the new kid's mouth?

"Cute," Todd said, as he finished his yawn with a forced little smile.

CUTE??! McGee wasn't cute! Clever, maybe. Imaginative, absolutely. But not *cute.* "Cute" was something you said when you couldn't think of anything good to say. "Cute" rated right up there with, "Nice," "Hmmmm," "Interesting," or "My, isn't that . . . unusual."

A sinking feeling started in Nick's stomach. He was mad, sure—but there was something else. Somewhere in the back of his brain a thought had started: Maybe that's all McGee really was. I mean, when compared to the talent that went into Jawbreaker, maybe McGee was just . . . "cute."

"Can I . . . can I see Jawbreaker again?" Nicholas croaked.

"Here," Todd said as he ripped the drawing out of his pad. "Look all you want."

He tossed the sketch to Nick, who just stood there with his mouth hanging open. Todd treated this incredible drawing of Jawbreaker like it was nothing. Like he could whip out one of those babies any old time.

Maybe he could.

"Thanks," Nicholas mumbled as Todd started to turn and head down the hall. Then, coming to his senses, Nick called, "Oh, uh, here. . . ." He carefully pulled out his sketch of McGee and handed it to Todd. Nick may have been stunned, but he knew his manners.

"Thanks," Todd said as he stuffed McGee into one of his books. If Nicholas's mouth was hanging open before, it was dragging on the floor now. Todd hadn't even looked at the drawing. He just stuffed it away like it was a piece of garbage.

"Can someone here tell me where the principal's office is?" Todd asked.

"C'mon, I'll show you." It was Louis again. What was he doing being so nice to the enemy? That traitor, that Benedict Arnold, that good-for-nothing turncoat. "You got any other drawings?" Louis asked as the two moved down the hall together.

"Yeah," the other kids chimed in, crowding around Todd as he headed down the hall. "You got any more? Does Jawbreaker fly, too? Is he as strong as he looks?"

The questions kept coming, but Nicholas didn't hear. He just stood there, silent and alone, watching the group move down the hall. Once again, he felt his ears start to burn. Once again, anger was growing inside him. And there was a strange sinking feeling in his gut. That wasn't just anger. What was going on? What were all these emotions roaring around inside him?

Nick looked down at the sketch of Jawbreaker in his hand. It was an awesome piece of art, he had to admit. Then, after taking in a deep breath, he slowly let it out. He wasn't sure what these new, strange feelings were, but one thing was certain: he didn't like them.

It was true that Nick was having a rough day,

but he wasn't alone. Little sister Jamie had a set of feelings to work out, too. Feelings centering around the fact that everybody in the Martin family was good at something. Nicholas had his drawing, Sarah had her ballet and singing, Grandma was good at her needlework and sewing, and Mom and Dad were good at . . . well, they were Mom and Dad, so they probably were good at everything.

There was just one little tiny problem. With everyone else being so good at things, there wasn't a whole lot left for Jamie to be good at. Oh, sure, everyone thought she was cute. But hey, "cute" only goes so far. To be honest, she was getting a little tired of being "the cutie," the little sister everyone comes up to wearing goofy smiles while patting her on the head. Dogs are for head-patting . . . not intelligent girls who are in the highest reading level of second grade!

Jamie had decided. It was time for her to be something . . . anything. She could hear it now. . . .

"There's Senator Jamie Martin running for President. . . ."

"There's Dr. Martin performing brain surgery. . . ."

"There's Miss Martin, the alligator tamer. . . ."

Anything at all. Anything, that is, but: "There's Jamie Martin, everybody's little sister. My, isn't she a cutie."

Jamie had thought this all out very carefully that afternoon at the outdoor ice rink. She would be something. She would be Jamie Martin, the world-famous figure skater (or ice hockey goalie—

she hadn't worked out the details yet).

Jamie glanced up. The sun was low in the sky. It was just dropping behind the bare oaks and maples that surrounded the park. Every winter about this time the city flooded this section of the park for people to skate on. It was a great place where there was something for everyone. The older kids were off to the left killing themselves trying to be speed skaters. Families and younger children were off to the right making a big, lazy oval. The oldtimers hovered near the burning trash barrels, trying to rub some warmth back into their bones.

Jamie blew out a breath. It was a cold afternoon. No doubt about it. She could see white puffs of smoke every time she breathed. In fact, her hands had only been out of her mittens a couple of minutes and they were already beginning to ache.

Nothing else about her was cold, though. No sir. That was the other disadvantage of being the youngest. No one would let you out of the house unless you were bundled up like a mummy. Two sets of everything, from socks to sweaters to underwear. *UNDERWEAR?!* Well, all right, *almost* everything. The point is, she was so roly-poly she felt like the Pillsbury Dough Boy. One thing was sure: she didn't have to worry about falling down on the ice. If she fell, she'd just roll right back up to her feet.

Which was a good thing, because falling was something she knew she'd be doing a lot of.

"Are you sure you don't want me to help?" Sarah had asked her earlier.

"No way!" Jamie had insisted. "You go with your friends. I'll be OK." She didn't bother to tell Sarah that this was something she *had* to do on her own. No one was going to help or baby her with this. No sir. If she was going to be somebody, she had to do it all by herself.

At last she finished lacing her skates. She slipped on her mittens, slowly stood up . . . and suddenly ended up face down on the ice. Yup, you guessed it, her feet had shot out from under her! She'd been roller-skating dozens of times, but this was different. Keeping her balance on those thin little blades was more like stilt-walking than roller-skating.

She tried again, and again she fell. And again. She wasn't even on the ice yet and she just kept falling! This was getting embarrassing.

At last she managed to stay up. Then slowly and ever so carefully she hobbled toward the ice. The frozen ground and packed snow did a lot to help her stay up. So did the passersby that she kept grabbing and hanging on to. Finally, she made it to the edge of the ice. Carefully, she set one foot on it . . . *Shhwitz-BOOM!* Her legs flew out, and she plunked down in a sitting position so hard that it made her teeth hurt.

There was some gentle laughter. She looked over her shoulder and saw Sarah gliding toward her with a smile. She had left her group of friends for a moment and was swooping in to help her.

"You OK, Munchkin?" Sarah asked, coming to a graceful stop beside her.

"Fine . . . ," Jamie muttered through clenched teeth. "I'm just fine."

"Here," Sarah said as she reached down to help. "Let me give you a—"

"I can do it on my own!" Jamie snapped.

"But maybe I can give you a few point—"

"I don't need your help. I'm fine!"

Sarah looked at her little sister. Usually she could figure out what was bothering Jamie. Not this time. "Is everything all right?" Sarah asked, a slightly worried frown on her face.

Jamie felt bad for being so mean, but she was also mad. Right now, the mad part was stronger. "I can do it myself . . . OK?" Her voice had a sharp edge to it.

"OK, fine," Sarah said. There was a sharpness coming into her voice, too. A sharpness that only older sisters know how to use on younger ones. A sharpness that says, *Hey, if you want to be a class-A jerk, don't let me stop you.* "Suit yourself," Sarah said, and with that she pushed off and glided effortlessly toward her friends.

Jamie sat and watched Sarah skate off. She was so graceful, so beautiful. In fact, everything about Sarah was beautiful—her hair, her eyes, her teeth . . . and now, her skating.

For a second, Jamie could feel tears welling up in her eyes. Was she jealous?

You'd better believe it.

Was she going to give up?

No way.

She would keep trying. She might not be as pretty as Sarah. Her teeth might not be as straight as Sarah's. But she was going to do something better than Sarah. She was going to be a skater . . . a great skater . . . the best skater that ever set a skate on the ice.

With that, Jamie drew a deep breath, gathered herself together, stood up . . . and fell flat again.

FOUR
And Grows . . .

For the past hour, Nick had been sitting in the family room trying to sketch Jawbreaker. By the zillion pieces of wadded up paper scattered about the room, it didn't look like he was having much success.

Every mark Nicholas made on his sketch pad seemed wrong. Every stroke of his pencil seemed to cry out, "Cute!" (He was really starting to hate that word.)

Still, instead of the powerful, high-tech lines that Todd used to draw Jawbreaker, Nick's version of the robot kept coming out sensitive, full of feeling, and looking, yes . . . cute.

"ARGHHHHH!" In anger, Nick tore out another piece of paper, wadded it up, and added it to the growing Mt. Trashmore at his feet.

Just across the room, sitting at the kitchen table, Nick's dad had his own fight on his hands. He was putting together a puzzle of the world. Not just any puzzle. We're talking five thousand pieces of puzzle. Five thousand eensy-weensy little pieces of puzzle that, after the past hour and a half, were all starting to look the same.

Nick's mom was over at the counter grating cheese. She could tell by the glassy look in her husband's eyes and the way he kept turning a puzzle piece over and over in his hands that the poor man needed help. She could also tell that there was no way he'd be finished in time for dinner.

"I thought you were going to move that mess to the family room," she said. "Or do we eat off the counter?"

Dad, who has never been known to admit defeat, answered, "You're looking at an expert at geographical puzzles, my dear. I'll be done in no time."

He laid a piece down in one of the empty spaces and tried to squeeze it in. It didn't quite fit. Maybe if he pushed a littler harder . . . a little harder still. Well, OK, maybe if he started pounding it with his fist. . . .

After the third bang on the table, Dad began to see reality. OK, maybe the piece from the Great Lakes would never pass for a part of the Pacific Ocean.

He glanced up to Mom, who was trying to hide her smile. "You can help . . . if you like," he offered.

"What a guy," she quipped. "Always willing to share your fun."

Handing her the worn and slightly broken piece of puzzle, Dad suggested, "Why not consider this a really cheap way to see Europe?"

With a grin, Mom pushed him over to the edge of the chair. "Move over, cheapskate," she said.

Meanwhile, back in the family room (which was

serving as Nick's personal torture chamber), the papers were still being wadded and thrown.

It was about this time that Sarah came bounding down the steps. She and Jamie had just come home from skating. . . . Well, skating for her. More like crashing and burning for Jamie.

"Look out, world!" she called as she saw her father at the table. "Dad's got a jigsaw puzzle."

"That's right," Dad said, busily destroying another piece. "And everyone who helps gets to sleep inside tonight."

Pulling up a chair, Sarah grinned. "Well, I'm not into igloos," she said, reaching out for a puzzle piece, "so count me in." She heard the rip of paper and looked over to see Nick destroying another sketch. "Hey!" she called out. "How come you're excused from helping?"

"I'm busy!" Nicholas snapped as he pitched the zillionth-and-a-half wad across the room.

Sarah could tell Nicholas was really bugged, so she did what any kind, considerate older sister would do. She bugged him some more. "Check it out," she called. "Rembrandt's busy."

Nick paid no attention.

"David," Mom said to Dad. "It may be a small world, but you can't substitute Paris, Texas for Paris, France."

"Well . . . ," Dad said, as he tossed the mutilated piece into the pile and grabbed another. "If you're going to be picky. . . ."

"Oh, I forgot about dinner!" Mom exclaimed. "Sarah? Would you grate some cheese?"

"Sure," she said. Then seeing Nick fighting with

another piece of paper, Sarah couldn't resist throwing another zinger his way. "Hey, Nick, you want to grate some cheese?"

Her timing was perfect. Nicholas ripped out the paper and angrily gathered up his things.

"I have work to do, OK?" he barked. "Can't you guys just leave me alone?!"

With that he stood up, stormed past her, and tromped up the stairs.

For a moment Sarah thought about feeling sorry for him. I mean, it was pretty obvious Nick was having a tough time. Then she got a hold of herself. After all, she *was* the older sister. Getting under your little brother's skin was expected. You couldn't really blame her, she was only doing her job.

I clutched the violin firmly under my ever-so-tuxedoed arm. Then, taking a deep breath, I peeked through the curtains out at the waiting audience. Ha! Just as I expected. The place was packed tighter than Roseanne's girdle. Well, why not. After all, they had come to see me, Adagio McGee, world renowned concert violinist and part-time vacuum cleaner salesman. I was about to perform at the world-famous Carnage Hall.

It was amazing. I had barely started my national tour (I'd played at Elmer's Bar and Grill, Bert Finglestein's Bar Mitzva, and Mrs. Snodgrass's Tupperware Party), but my reputation was spreading faster than a bad case of athlete's foot.

The crowd out there was already going wild. Some were chanting, "McGee, McGee, McGee!" while the rest were hooting and hollering. I mean, everyone was doing everything they could to keep me from playing. But, hey, I paid good money for all their tickets. I was entitled to play at least a couple of tunes.

Then I heard it, the announcer's voice over the speakers: "And now ladies and gentlemen . . . direct from Eastfield, the entertainment capital of the world . . . Heeeeeeeerrrrrre's McGee!!"

I stepped out onto the stage. My reception was underwhelming. The lack of applause was deafening. Obviously these people had never seen a musical genius with such intensely handsome features. Then it began: thousands of fans began to clap. Well, OK, maybe it was hundreds. Would you believe a dozen? OK, OK, so this one person clapped, and she only clapped one time . . . but one clap was enough. I smiled a knowing smile, glad that Mom could make it.

Now, at center stage, I raised the violin to my chin. The audience gasped. I glanced around the auditorium. No one was breathing. They were all holding their breath in anticipation (either that or they were trying to pass out so they'd miss my performance).

I raised the bow to the strings and began. It was a fantastic flourish of fortitude as my fabulous fingers flew across the strings. I had no idea what I was playing, but it must have been great because everyone's eyes were starting to water. The music was filled with such emotion that there wasn't a dry eye in the house. It was so moving that even the dogs outside the theater were starting to howl and cry.

Then, just when I was ready to let loose and really show them my stuff, Nicholas threw open his bedroom door. Suddenly the concert hall was gone, and I was once again in his bedroom, and my stage once again became his drawing table. Rats! Another one of my great fantasies wrecked by Nicholas Martin's reality. Oh well, I still had the toy violin.

Nick slammed the door and stalked over to his beanbag chair. I could tell by the expression on his face that things weren't going so well (either that, or he was sucking on lemon slices again).

I gave another fantastic flourish on my fiddle to brighten his day. He showed his appreciation by barking out, "What are you doing?"

"Just fiddling around," I grinned. My humorous humor always humors up his humorless moods.

"Will you knock it off?!" he growled.

Well, so much for "always."

"You're just jealous," I shouted over my perfect performance, "because all you can play is the radio!"

"I am not jealous!" Nicholas yelled.

"Yeah, right. That's why you've been trying to draw that bucket of bolts all night."

"Hey," Nick said, looking surprised. "I was just messing around."

"I'll say," I smirked. "Trying to draw that two-ton toaster is obviously gonna be a mess."

"Look . . .," he growled. (No doubt about it, ol' Nicky-boy wasn't a happy camper. I must have hit a nerve talking about this newfangled tin man.) "I've never drawn that type of stuff before," he said somewhere between a snarl and a whine. "I mean, it's got all those lines and angles and things. . . ."

41

I could tell Nick was throwing one of his world-famous pity parties. He didn't hold them often, but when he did they were beauts. I mean, people would come from miles around just to sit and watch him feel sorry for himself. (Of course, the chips and dips were pretty good, too.)

Anyway, knowing we were heading down "Woe-is-Me Lane," I did what any best buddy in the world would do. I started playing some sappy, tear-jerking music on my violin. Hey, it fit his sappy, tear-jerking story.

It did the trick, too. Instead of whining, he started to get mad again. "I don't care if Todd can draw. I mean, he can draw what he draws. Besides, what's the big deal around here? A guy tries to change what he draws and everybody makes a federal case out of it." Suddenly he realized what I was up to, and he spun around and snapped, "OK, Nero, knock it off!"

I ended with one of my more dramatic endings, then quietly lowered the violin. It was time to get serious. My little friend was definitely hurting; there was no doubt about it. Whether he knew it or not, he was definitely filled with one thing and one thing only: Jealousy.

"It's really getting to you, isn't it?" I said.

Sensing my concern and care, Nick answered with equal sensitivity.

"Yeah, well, it wouldn't be such a bad idea to trade you in for a robot, Mop Top!"

With that, he stormed out of the room. Well, so much for care and sensitivity. In fact, his answer was so sharp that it cut one of my violin strings . . . TWEEENK-BOING!

I stood in silence for a long moment. Things were tougher for Nick than I thought. Jealousy's a terrible thing, the way it can eat into a person—making you angry and scared and prideful all at the same time. And Nick had it bad . . . real bad.

FIVE
And Grows Some More

Everything in the school library was quiet. Well, almost everything. Nicholas's thoughts were anything but quiet. In fact, if you could have crawled inside his head you would have heard all sorts of shoutings and yellings and screamings. And they all had to do with one Todd Burton and his ominous creation, Jawbreaker.

I'm better than he is!

I'll never be as good as he is!

What a stupid drawing. That robot has no heart! No feeling!

Why does all my stuff have to have so much heart and feeling?

McGee's better than Jawbreaker ever thought of being!

If I could just get McGee to look a little more like Jawbreaker. . . .

And so the arguments roared inside Nick's head. Along with lots of feelings. One minute Nick was mad, the next afraid. He was full of pride, then he thought he was worthless. It was like a nonstop merry-go-round. Around and around this stuff churned in his mind. It was awful.

Until, that is, Nicholas came out from behind the bookshelves and saw Todd drawing at a nearby table, surrounded by all of the kids. Then it was worse than awful.

Suddenly they broke out in laughter. Nicholas tried to ignore them. After all, he was there to find a book for a book report, not join Todd's new fan club. But the giggles and snickers were too much to resist. Before he knew it, Nick had joined the crowd. And I do mean "crowd." There were so many kids there that he couldn't even get in to see what Todd was drawing. Then Nick spotted Louis and moved

next to him. "What's so funny?" he asked.

Louis looked up. The grin on his face slowly froze. He didn't say a word.

Puzzled, Nick turned from his friend and looked back toward the table. One of the kids had moved just far enough for him to catch a glimpse of the drawing, and he finally saw the reason for everyone's laughter.

There was Jawbreaker on Todd's sketch pad. He was as high-tech and tough as ever. Nothing funny about that. What *was* funny was the way he was throwing a squirming little creature into the trash can. When Nick looked closer he saw that the squirming little creature just happened to be . . . McGee!

Nick sucked in his breath. What was McGee doing on Todd's pad?!

By now Todd had noticed Nick standing there. "I'm just goofing off," Todd smirked. "Drawing this McGee clown isn't that hard, especially if you've had any kind of training."

Nick could only stare. Not only had Todd drawn his usually awesome Jawbreaker, but he had also drawn a pretty good version of McGee!

It felt as if someone had slugged Nick in the stomach. McGee was his! *He* had created him. *He* had sweated over him. *He* had poured all of his imagination into the little guy. And now . . . now some new kid creep was coming in, slapping him down on his sketch pad, and saying anybody could draw him.

Nick wanted to grab Todd by the collar and pull him to his feet. He wanted to shout him down into a quivering mass of protoplasm. He wanted to clobber him again and again and again until Todd cried for mercy—until he admitted that McGee was Nick's, and only Nick's, and that nobody could draw like Nicholas Martin!

That's what Nick wanted to do . . . but he knew he couldn't do any of it. Actually, he probably *could*, but he wouldn't. Nobody would do those sort of things.

"Who wants to give me fifty cents?" Derrick Cryder called as he pushed his way into the crowd.

Well, almost nobody.

Nick glanced at the big kid almost hopefully as he approached Todd. But Derrick was not in a punching mood. Instead, he took one look at the drawing, laughed, and then turned to Nicholas. "How come you can't draw like that, Martin?"

Nick opened his mouth, but no words came out. Derrick didn't pay any attention. He had already found some poor little kid who was rapidly agreeing that he would be more than happy to go without buying lunch today.

As all eyes turned to watch Derrick terrorize the kid, Louis leaned over and whispered to Nicholas. "Hey, don't take it so hard. That drawing's just a joke."

A joke? Is that what he called it?? If Louis thought that was a joke, he must have thought World War II was hilarious, the Black Plague hysterical, and dropping the H-bomb a real sidesplitter!

Nick wanted to say all of those things, but again he didn't. Instead, he just stared at the picture and quietly croaked, "Yeah . . . real funny."

"OK, everyone." It was Mrs. Harmon. "Time to head back to class. Did you all pick out a book for your reports?"

Derrick, who had just scored his fifty cents (plus a new Paper Mate pen as a bonus), suddenly realized he'd forgotten to get a book. Being the true-blue bully he was, he reached toward Renee and quickly grabbed one of the books out of her hands.

"I've got my book," he beamed to Mrs. Harmon in his best Eddie Haskel imitation.

"I see," said Mrs. Harmon as she took it from him and read the title out loud. *"Pretty and Popular: The Modern Girl's Guide to Good Looks.* I'll be interested to see what you have to write on this subject, Derrick."

A couple of the kids snickered. That is, until Derrick nailed them with his death stare.

"Oh, Nick," Mrs. Harmon called. "Did you see this on the bulletin board? It's something you might be interested in." She reached out and handed a copy of a flier to him. "The Eastfield Winter Carnival is having a poster contest. The winning entry will be posted all over town and printed in the paper."

Nick could feel his chest start to swell a little. Well, at least *somebody* in the school knew who the real artist was.

"Thanks, Mrs. Harmon!" He said as he glanced proudly to the other students. *There,* he thought to himself. *I guess that shows you guys. . . .*

"Oh, and Todd . . . " It was Mrs. Harmon again.

Suddenly there was that sinking feeling in Nick's stomach again.

"I hear you're a pretty good artist too," she said as she handed him a flier. "You'll probably also want to enter."

"Thanks," Todd said, grabbing the flier and giving it a quick glance. "Might be fun."

Nicholas continued to stare at the new kid in disbelief. Fun? Fun??! This was going to be anything but "fun."

Later, the class was back in Mrs. Harmon's room. The blinds were closed and the lights were off. She was showing slides of Renaissance Art. Up on the screen was a picture of the Sistine Chapel—the one where God's hand is reaching out to touch Adam's. It's a great piece of art, and Nicholas tried his best to pay attention, but his mind kept drifting back to Todd and the contest.

"Now, who can name one of the most famous artists from the Renaissance?" Mrs. Harmon was asking.

Nicholas didn't know and didn't care. Todd, on the other hand . . .

"Michelangelo!" he shouted.

"No, it's da Vinci." Renee argued.

"Very good. You're both right," Mrs. Harmon said, beaming.

Todd beamed right back.

Oh, brother, Nicholas thought as he rolled his eyes away from the new kid. *It's one thing for Renee to have the right answer—she always does. But now Toddy-boy here thinks he's an art historian, too. Give me a break.*

"In fact," Mrs. Harmon continued, "Leonardo da

Vinci and Michelangelo were both brilliant. They had quite a jealous rivalry going on between them for many years."

Mrs. Harmon kept rambling on, but Nick was no longer listening. He had heard something about "jealousy" and "rivalry." That's all it took. Once again he was starting to drift into one of his fantasies. The type that usually involve McGee. Only there was no McGee in this one. This time it was just Nicholas.

What if he were Michelangelo? Hmmm. . . .

And what if Todd was Leonardo da Vinci? Double hmmm. . . .

Nick looked around. He was in a huge Renaissance hall! Music was playing, and everyone was dressed like something out of Romeo and Juliet. Nick glanced down at himself. The rich velvet clothing was pretty impressive . . . though he could have done without the tights. Oh well, it was only a daydream. Who was going to see him in a daydream?

"Gentlemen . . ."

Nick looked up. There was a pompous sort of twit sitting behind a massive table full of food. By the way he was dressed (and by the way he was picking his teeth), it was pretty obvious he was the head honcho.

"On behalf of myself, the Duke of Ellington, and my Vice Regent, Sir Loin of Beef . . ." He motioned to a big hunk of flesh who was sitting beside him and chowing down on an even bigger hunk of turkey leg. "I welcome you to the competition for the painting of the Pristine Chapel."

There was a loud fanfare by the local minstrel,

50

who was an even twittier twit than the first guy. He was playing a lute. Unfortunately, Nicholas had never actually heard a lute, so his imagination made the guy sound a lot like Jimi Hendrix at Woodstock.

The Duke of Ellington cleared his throat angrily. Obviously he had never heard Jimi Hendrix. The minstrel stopped. Finally the Duke turned to Nicholas with a gracious nod. *"Nick*elangelo . . ."

Nick returned the nod.

"And *Todd*onardo da Vinci."

Surprised, Nick turned to see Todd standing beside him. He was dressed in a similar outfit. Hey! What was the deal here? Couldn't Nicholas even have a daydream without Todd barging in?

Before Nick could protest, the Duke continued. "Which one of you will present a sample of your work first?"

Nick narrowed his eyes. Now it was all becoming clear. He and Todd were each standing in front of a covered painting. Of course! They must be competing for the right to paint the Pristine Chapel. *Well, here goes nothing,* Nicholas thought as he started to open his mouth. But before he could speak, Todd jumped in.

"Your most royal, grand, exalted, incredibly excellent Duke-a-tude."

Nicholas rolled his eyes. The kid was obviously laying it on way too thick. Anybody could see that. Well, almost anybody. . . .

"Ooooo, he's good," the Duke crooned, grinning at his snorting sidekick. "He's *very* good."

"Here's a little portrait," Todd continued, "that I

51

whipped up this morning over breakfast." With that he pulled the cover off of the painting to reveal an oil painting of the Mona Lisa! "I call it, 'The Moaning Lisa.'"

The crowd gasped in astonishment. So did Nick.

"Stupendous . . . wonderful . . . fabulous!" the Duke exclaimed. "By the way, do you do business cards? Something not too flashy, with a royal sort of flair. I mean, I'm looking for—" He was so impressed that he completely forgot Nick. He went on and on about business stationery and letterheads and—

"Hey! What about me?" Nicholas finally interrupted.

"Oh . . . yes." The Duke turned to him a little irritated. "Very well, proceed, Nickelangelo . . . if you must."

OK, not the most enthusiastic response. But Nick was on. This was his big chance.

"Sir," Nick said, giving none of the false flattery or fakey praise Todd had given. Just polite respect. The Duke would obviously appreciate that type of honesty.

"A poor start," the Duke muttered to his overstuffed friend. "A very poor start."

Sir Loin grunted in response and reached for a nearby lamb leg.

Nicholas continued. "I envision a magnificent painting that would capture the magnificence of the creation of the entire world!" There, *that* should get their attention. And it did. With a confident smile, he continued. "Thus, I think you will agree when you see my sketches, that I should paint the Pristine Chapel."

It was quite a buildup. All eyes were glued to Nick's covered painting. Nick wasn't worried. After all, this was his daydream. With a flair he reached for the cover and quickly whisked it aside. There was his masterpiece.

Nick looked at the Duke and Sir Loin, waiting for their expressions of delight and amazement. Instead, they burst out laughing. Stunned, Nick looked at them, then down at his brilliant artwork.

It was a clumsy stick figure.

A stick figure?! Wait a minute, what was going on?? *What's wrong with this stupid fantasy, anyway??* Nick thought angrily.

"Er, um, very nice," the Duke coughed, trying not to choke on his laughter. "Yes, well, perhaps we'll give you a call . . . ," he paused to think a moment. "When we need to paint . . . the basement."

"Wait!" Nick cried. "This isn't my best stuff!" He was in a panic. "Just give me a—"

But the Duke had already turned to Todd. "Toddonardo, when can you begin?"

"Wait a minute!" Nicholas shouted. "I can do better than him. Give me another chance! I can do better. I can do better!!"

Mrs. Harmon stopped her lecture and turned to Nick with a puzzled look on her face. "You think you can do better than Leonardo da Vinci, Nick?"

Suddenly, the daydream was gone. Nick looked around. He was back in his classroom. What's more, he was standing up. And everyone was staring at him. He had been so desperate to convince the Duke that he hadn't realized he had been shouting out loud.

Of course, the kids all laughed and slapped him on the back. And, of course, Nick did his best to try to melt into his seat. But there was no way to disappear.

Great, Nick thought to himself. *Just great.*

He glanced over at Todd who was laughing with the rest of the kids. Well, why shouldn't Todd laugh? He had nothing to lose. I mean, let's face it, he was better than Nicholas . . . even in Nick's own daydreams.

SIX
Let the Competition Begin

Later that afternoon, little Jamie was back at the
park and out on the ice. She planned to be out
there every day for the rest of her life . . . or until she
could beat Sarah at skating, whichever came first.

She had finally mastered the fine art of standing
without falling. The next step was to stand and
skate at the same time. She wasn't sure how to go
about it, but over the past hour and a half she had
a pretty good idea how *not* to do it. I mean, any way
you could think of to fall, Jamie had tried it.

Now she was standing at the edge of the pond,
holding onto a nearby tree. She'd been doing a lot
of that . . . grabbing things. Usually they were
people passing by. And usually both she and the
person she grabbed would go crashing onto the ice.
It didn't take too long for her to build a reputation.
In fact, it was getting kind of embarrassing to hear,
"Look out, it's Jamie!" or, "Quick everybody, move
over! Jamie Martin's coming my way!!"

OK, so it was time to try something different.

Now she had her trusty tree. If she could just sort of push off and glide across the ice, maybe no one would notice that she wasn't really skating. Of course, this style might not get her into the Winter Olympics, but at least it was something. And some style was better than no style . . . or so she thought.

She hung onto the tree and watched as Sarah and her friends passed by. As usual, they were laughing and having a good old time. *That's OK,* Jamie thought. *Let them laugh. I'll show them. I'll show them all.*

With that, she clenched her jaws tightly and pushed off from the tree. . . .

At first everything went beautifully. Then she noticed her feet starting to drift apart. Further and further they drifted. As hard as she tried, she couldn't stop them. They just kept spreading. She had never done the splits before and really didn't want to start now. But, like it or not, it looked like she was going to get her chance.

Then she heard it . . . laughter. It was coming from behind her and to the left. Without a moment's hesitation she reached out. Her timing couldn't have been better. She managed to grab onto a passerby's arm. Unfortunately, that passerby had just grabbed onto someone else, who had just grabbed onto someone else, who had . . . well, I think you get the picture. Without knowing it, Jamie had become the end of a giant chain of skaters who were playing Crack the Whip.

Now, as you may know, the object of Crack the Whip is to get the person on the end whipping around so fast that he can't hang on anymore, so he goes flying off out of control. Guess who was now that fortunate, soon-to-be-airborne end person? You got it: Jamie.

Back and forth she went. Faster and faster. People were a blur. Trees were a blur. Come to think of it, *everything* was a blur. All Jamie could remember was someone screaming. Someone who sounded an awful lot like her!

Finally she couldn't hold on any longer. She went flying off the end at what felt like a hundred miles an hour. People scrambled out of her way, scooping up their children, diving for cover as she shot past them.

Then she saw it—her trusty tree, right in front of her and coming up . . . fast. She had no choice. She did what any clear thinking, all-star world-class athlete would do. She screamed her lungs out.

"AHHHHHHHHHHHHHHHHHhhhhhhhhhhhh!!"

That must have been what it took. She missed the tree by just a few inches and plowed into the soft white snow bank. She was lucky. Soft, white snow banks tend to cause fewer headaches (and broken bones) than hard tree trunks.

Immediately, Sarah was at her side, digging her out, helping her to her feet. "Are you OK?" she kept asking. "Is everything all right?"

Finally Jamie looked up and did her best attempt at a smile. "I think so. . . ."

Sarah sighed in relief. "Boy, you sure had me worried."

Jamie nodded. She'd had herself worried too. But she also had an idea. "Sarah?" she asked.

"Yeah?"

"Maybe . . . maybe I'm not cut out to be a figure skater." Sarah gently helped her sister to her feet as she continued. "Maybe . . . maybe I should be a speed skater!"

When Sarah and Jamie got home, Dad once again was lost in the jigsaw puzzle. Sure, he was supposed to be getting ready to go to some concert with Mom. But Mom was out of the room, so he figured he could sneak in a couple more pieces.

Jamie peeled off her layers of coats and jumped in to help, along with Sarah and Grandma.

"David," Mom groaned as she entered the room. "I told you half an hour ago . . ."

"I know, I know," Dad said. "I just need Mada-gascar."

Mom let out a long sigh. The type that husbands are supposed to hear and respond to immediately if they're paying any attention, which, of course, Dad wasn't. Resigned, Mom reached for What-ever's bowl and began filling it with dog food. "Here you go, Whatever. Come here, boy."

The little furball scampered into the kitchen and began chowing down for all he was worth. Mom looked at Dad again.

"David, the concert's at eight!"

"Right," Dad answered. He dropped in another piece and quickly crossed out of the room to get his coat.

"Men!" Mom groaned as she started to pace the kitchen.

"Oh, come on," Grandma said. "Sit down for a second."

With another one of her wifely sighs, Mom slumped into the nearby kitchen chair. Without really meaning to, she glanced at the puzzle. Im-mediately, she spotted a fit. "What about this piece here?" she asked as she reached for it, then quickly plopped it into place.

That was all it took. Mom was hooked. Suddenly the concert was a million miles away. Nick, on the other hand, wasn't.

He stormed into the room and tossed his sketch pad on the counter. "Mom . . . ," he whined impa-tiently. He was still a little bugged about Todd, Mrs. Harmon, the contest . . . everything. "Are we *ever* going to eat around here?"

OK, better make that a *lot* bugged. His mind was churning with thoughts. No one respected his talent. Not Todd, not the kids . . . and now, not even Mrs. Harmon. Well, maybe that was only right. Maybe he didn't have any talent to respect.

"MOM!"

But Mom barely heard. "We'll eat in a little while," she said, as she fit another piece in. "Why don't you fix yourself a little snack and come help?"

The last thing in the world Nick felt like doing was joining the jigsaw junkies. Instead, he made all the noise he could as he opened and closed the fridge, then slammed various drawers and cupboards. But no one was paying him any attention.

Typical, he thought. *Just like at school.*

"I got Misery!" Jamie shouted triumphantly as she held up a piece.

"That's Missouri," Sarah corrected.

Dad whisked into the room. "I'm ready. Let's get going."

"In a minute," Mom answered.

"But you were the one who said we had to—"

"Mom!" Nick interrupted. "There's no cookies, no peanut butter, no crackers!"

"Here," Grandma said, shoving another puzzle piece into Mom's hand. "Try this one."

"I suppose I could eat some baking soda!" Sarcasm was one of Nick's better talents, but even that didn't seem to get anyone's attention.

"Just don't stuff yourself," Mom answered absentmindedly.

"Gee," Nick whined as he looked over to

Whatever. "Maybe I'll just have a nice bowl of Kibbles 'n Bits."

"I told you, dear, whatever you want. . . . Oh, and please take your junk off the counter."

By now Dad had pulled off his coat and once again joined the team. "Hand me some of those pieces, will you?"

"Junk is right!" Nicholas said scornfully, looking at his sketch pad. A lot of good that stupid pad had done him these last couple of days. In fact, it seemed to be nothing but a source of pain and embarrassment for him. Then, without even thinking what he was doing, he scooped up the pad and stormed toward the garbage can under the sink. He opened the cupboard doors and stood there staring at the garbage. And as he stood there, he remembered. . . .

Some of the best times he'd had were spent over that sketch pad. This was the pad where he had created McGee. This was the pad where he had drawn all of those great adventures. This was the pad where the two of them had worked out so many problems together. Now . . .

Now maybe it was all just a joke. Maybe he really couldn't draw. I mean, that's what everybody else seemed to think. At least when they compared him to Todd Burton. OK. That was fine and dandy with him. If they didn't think he could draw, he wouldn't draw. Plain and simple. "This will show them," he muttered under his breath. "This will show them all!"

With one quick motion, he pitched the pad into the garbage.

K-THOOMP!

Nick stood there another moment letting it sink in. That was it. That was the end of his drawing career. Just like that. Nicholas Martin was no longer an artist. The world would just have to get along without his masterpieces. He would find another hobby. Maybe mountain climbing. Maybe scuba diving. But he was no longer going to draw. Ever.

He stared at the pad lying there in the garbage. It was lifeless and unmoving. Nick felt a tightness in his chest and throat. He swallowed hard, fighting the emotions that welled up inside of him. This was one of the hardest things he had ever done—and no one had even noticed. No one had heard.

He glanced over at the table. They were still hovering over the puzzle. *Typical,* he thought, angry tears filling his eyes. Then, slamming the cupboard door, he turned and stomped up the stairs to his room. *Why should anyone notice?* he asked himself. *Why should anyone care?*

But Nick was wrong. Someone did notice . . . and care.

Several minutes later Nicholas was sitting at his window quietly watching the snow fall. He could feel the ache starting somewhere in the back of his throat again. How could things have gotten so bad so quickly? Two days ago he was top dog, cream of the crop, Mr. Nobody-Can-Draw-as-Good-as-Me. Now . . . now he was pond scum.

The ache in his throat was growing worse. He tried to swallow it back, but it did no good. If he wasn't careful, his eyes would start burning and those darned tears would try to sneak out. He hated it when that happened. Luckily, he had a visitor before things got out of hand.

"Here's your Kibbles 'n Bits," he heard a voice say.

He turned to see Grandma smiling in the doorway. She was holding Whatever's food dish. It was piled high with dog food.

He tried to smile back but wasn't too successful.

Grandma had seen it all. She had seen Nick's attitude when he stormed into the kitchen. She had seen him throw his sketch pad away. Now she saw him trying to hold back the tears and ignore the ache in his throat. Without a word she crossed the room and sat beside him. Finally, after several moments, she spoke.

"What's going on?"

"Nothing," he lied.

"Nick . . . ," her voice was strong and determined. "I'm not leaving this seat until you tell me what's the matter." Grandma was a sweet old lady—but she was a tough sweet old lady. I mean, working thirty years as a missionary in Central America is bound to give you a little strength. Usually, when she made up her mind about something, there was no changing it. And it was pretty obvious she had made up her mind about this.

Poor Nick. It didn't look like he had much choice. It was time to resort to the old stall tactic. "I don't know. . . ." One look at Grandma said she wasn't buying that, either. He would have to tell her everything. So, with a deep breath, he began. "There's this new kid in school and he draws, and all of a sudden everyone thinks he's a great artist. . . ."

"You mean all of this stewing is because of a new kid at school?" Her tone had softened a little.

"But Grandma, this guy, Todd . . . he blows into town and he really acts like a creep. And everybody treats him like he's so great."

There was a long pause before Grandma finally spoke. Her voice was quiet and thoughtful. "Nick, do you think there's a possibility that you're . . . jealous?"

Jealous?! What'd he have to be jealous about? He was better than Todd ever thought of being. Well, at least that's what part of him thought. The other part was scared to death that Todd was better . . . a lot better.

"Sweetie," Grandma put her hand on his leg and continued. "Did you really think there was nobody in the world who could draw as well as you?"

"Well, no . . . ," Nicholas stammered. He knew there were better artists around. No doubt. He just didn't expect to wind up sitting across the aisle from one.

"Honey . . . ," Grandma's voice was kind, but there was no missing that firmness again. "The Lord gave you your ability to draw to honor *him* . . . not to honor you."

Nick started to open his mouth, but he had no answer. What could he say? From the time he could remember, his parents had encouraged him to live his life for God, not for himself. A few years back he had decided to do just that. He had given his life to Jesus Christ.

Actually, when you stop to think about it, it was a pretty good idea—giving his life to Jesus, that is. Nick agreed to let Jesus be his boss. In return, Jesus would love him, protect him, watch over him, and open the way for him to get into heaven. Not a bad deal.

Still, as Grandma said, if Nick had really given his life to Jesus, he had also given him his talents. Which meant his talents were for Jesus' glory, not his.

Grandma wasn't finished. "Who do you think you're going to punish by giving up your drawing?" she asked. "Not Todd."

"But Grandma . . . ," Nick could feel his voice growing thick with emotion. "I just . . . I just don't feel like drawing anymore."

Grandma nodded silently. It was like she understood—really understood. Maybe she did.

After another long pause, she said, "Nicholas, before your Grandpa and I were sent to the mission field, we lost a wonderful position to another missionary couple. We were so jealous we couldn't see straight."

Nick looked up in astonishment. His grandparents had been jealous? This perfect couple who had done all of these great things for God? They had actually been . . . jealous?

Grandma saw the look on his face and chuckled before continuing. "But when we got to know that couple . . . well, we realized how much we had in common."

Nick looked at her curiously. "Maybe . . . ," she finished, "Maybe you should focus on what you and Todd have in *common* rather than on your jealousy."

She let the idea sink in for a long moment. Then, giving him another gentle pat on the knee, she slowly stood up.

Nick watched silently as she headed for the door and went out into the hall. She had a point. It had been fun being the only cartoonist in school . . . but it had also been kind of lonely. Now there was someone who had the same interests Nick did. Maybe they could become friends. Maybe they could even work together and learn from each other.

Suddenly Nick's sketch pad came flying back into the room! Apparently Grandma had dug it out of the trash. "Now get to work!" she shouted.

Nick broke into a grin. Grandma had made her point. If *she* could admit to having been jealous, it was OK for *him* to admit he was jealous. But he was going to do more than admit it. He was going to get rid of it. He wasn't going to let it control him any longer. He was tired of letting it make him do things he didn't want to do, of letting it gnaw away at him. From now on, he was going to take charge.

With a growing determination, he rose from the chair, picked up his sketch pad, and started to think. There must be something he could draw for the poster contest. . . .

SEVEN
The Showdown

Boy, oh boy, that was closer than a punk rocker's haircut. I tell you, if Grandma hadn't done her little search and rescue job in the ol' garbage can I might still be there enjoying the fragrant aromas of coffee grounds, egg shells, and the ever-popular 'Eau de spoiling cottage cheese.' (Kinda makes your mouth water just thinking about it, doesn't it?)

Thanks to Grandma, I was back. And just in time, too. I was needed desperately to help my little buddy come up with a winning idea for the Winter Carnival poster. What better person was there to help than me, the magnificently minded McGee?

Before Nick knew it, I had changed into my world-famous ice hockey uniform. Holy hockey puck! Of course! Who could represent the Winter Carnival better than me, poised for action with my hockey stick and my disarmingly handsome smile? A second later, though, my smile got disarmed when a hockey puck came flying in from nowhere and did a little free dental work on my teeth. (Actually, a lot of free dental work.) Well, at least now I won't have to worry about brushing after meals.

I glanced up at Nick. He was shaking his head.

OK, fine. He didn't like hockey. How 'bout . . . I did another quick twirl (the type only contagiously cute cartoon characters can do) and BINGO! I was now clad in my world-famous figure skater outfit.

I looked around. The grandstands were full of cheering (or is that jeering?) spectators. They all wanted one thing: me off the ice. Yes, there I was in the middle of the Winter Olympics skating my little heart out. And I was great! The crowd was already on its feet (and racing for the doors). The music grew to a feverish pace as I raised my stupen-dously sculptured leg and gracefully skated back-wards for the grand finale. Everyone began to gasp and shout and point. Obviously they had never seen such grace and skill—either that, or they saw the upcoming wall, which I suddenly shish-ka-bobbed with my raised skate.

Now I was stuck . . . and I do mean stuck. I was a permanent part of the arena, my leg gracefully but permanently raised behind me. Now don't get me wrong, this wouldn't be a bad position if you wanted to retire as a hood ornament. I just wasn't ready for retirement; I still had a couple of discount coupons for miniature golf and some last-minute Christmas shopping to do.

Luckily, Nick had another idea. . . .

Suddenly I was at the summit of a tall mountain top. The wind whipped at my scarf as I carefully adjusted the goggles over my beautiful baby blues. Before me lay the highest ski jump known to man.

That's OK. I was the greatest ski jumper known to man. I took a deep breath, dug my ski poles in, and pushed off. I roared down the ramp, but as I shot off the end I suddenly noticed Nicholas had forgotten to draw skis on my feet.

"NICHOLAS . . . !"

I began tumbling and falling out of control.

"Picky, picky, picky," Nick's voice said, as his pencil quickly appeared to draw an enormous bird right below me. I landed on its back and grabbed a fistful of feathers as we gently glided down to earth.

I hopped off my fowl-feathered friend and was about to give Nick a piece of my mind (a dangerous thing to do for those of us with so little mind to start out with) when I noticed he was grinning from ear to ear. All right! He finally had an idea. It was about time. This creative business can get a little dangerous for us cartoon types.

Now that Nick had his idea, he began to sketch it on a large piece of poster board. When he had everything all laid out, he began to outline it more darkly.

Next came the coloring.

He worked on it for several hours that night, and during lunch hour the following day. By the end of school he was finished. He held it up and smiled in satisfaction. There was McGee, perched high atop a beautiful mountain (this time with skis). At the bottom, in colorful, bright letters, the slogan read:

"The Eastfield Winter Carnival . . . It's Tops!"

It was one of Nick's better drawings. He was

more than a little pleased as he handed it in to the librarian.

"Hey, doofus . . . let's see your poster of McGeek!" Of course, it was Derrick. He was also handing in a poster. Nick didn't pay too much attention. He had done the best he could, and that was all that counted. The little talk with Grandma had really done the trick. He wasn't drawing to please Derrick, the kids, or even himself. He was now drawing to please God.

Later, as he passed Todd in the hall, he barely felt the jealousy that had been so strong the night before. Oh, it was still there, but there was a lot less than yesterday. And as the days continued to pass, the jealousy would continue to disappear.

Still, the war wasn't entirely over . . . not just yet. The librarian had hung the boys' posters side-by-side on the bulletin board. Later, after every one had gone home, McGee and Jawbreaker had some time to, well, work out their own differences . . . in their own special kind of way. . . .

Now that my little buddy was finally getting things straight with Todd, I figured the least I could do was try and be friends with the other new kid on my block . . . Jawbreaker. So, after we both hopped off of our posters, I offered ol' Metal Mouth my best handshake.

Unfortunately, the bucket of bolts had other ideas.

Before you can shout, "Incoming!" a mechanical flyswatter the size of Hulk Hogan's ego shot out of Jawbreaker's arm and slapped down right in front of me. Fortunately being in my superior athletic shape, I managed to leap out of the way just in time.

"Hey!" I shouted. "Why don't you cool off, Heater Head!"

The guy obviously thought I was the one who needed cooling off. A giant torrent of water suddenly roared out of his other arm.

Now I like taking a little swim as much as the next guy. But not in the middle of winter. And not after spending two and a half hours fixing my hair. (I know what you're thinking, but it was a busy day, and two and a half hours was all I could squeeze in.)

The water just kept coming. For a second I thought of looking for a bar of soap, maybe some shampoo—I could always work in a little shower. But all Hose Head had was a dried-up tube of Head 'n Shoulders. Since super heroes never have dandruff, I grabbed my umbrella, warbled out a quick chorus of "Singing in the Rain," and split faster than a pair of generic jeans.

It did no good. Ol' Bolt Brain was right on my tail. Now he began firing something out of his other arm. I wasn't too concerned. After all, this is a kid's book, so it couldn't be anything too dangerous. Then his little "presents" connected, and I realized I was getting a very pointed message . . . with cactuses. That's right. Little, round, very prickly cactuses. Believe me, I got the point. In more ways than one.

"YEOWWWW . . . KOOOW-AAAA-BUNG-GAAAAAAA!" (Translation: This has been lots of fun guys, but I don't think I'm going to stick around for an encore.)

Faster than you can say "Turn on the afterburners!" I was out of there. The metal moron came to a screeching halt. I was nowhere to be found. Of course, I didn't want him to feel left out. After all, we were getting to be such good friends. So I raced back onto the scene with a basketball. If he wants to play games, we'll play games.

"Hey, Sport!" I shouted. "How about a little 'one-on-one'?"

Jawbreaker watched with awe as I did some dynamically dramatic dribbling. Back and forth. Forth and back. But what's a basketball game without some play-by-play commentary? Since the titanium troll wasn't real talkative, I figured (here it comes . . .) the ball was in my court. (All right! All right! Stop the groaning.)

"And Magic McGee dribbles around the defense!" I shouted dramatically. "The Chromium Clod does his best to guard the basket but he's no match for McGee's fabulous fleet feet. McGee sets up . . . he looks for an open shot. . . ."

By now the hunk of junk was pretty excited. I mean, he wanted the ball and he wanted it bad. So, I did what any loving, caring, superstar type person would do: I gave it to him. The look on his face was full of thanks and appreciation. I almost felt bad when the ball opened and a giant boxing glove sprang out, and whomped him smack dab in the snoot.

It didn't seem to slow him down, though. He just shook it off and came racing toward me. OK, so I guess we weren't quite done with our afternoon workout.

74

"All right, Bucket Brain!" I shouted, as I grabbed a nearby pole-vaulting pole. "Stick 'em up!"

I tossed the pole toward him and he caught it on the run. He looked a little confused as the other end of the pole wobbled, then dug into the ground, bent for a moment, and shot him 3.8 jillion miles into the air and over the bar. Actually, he set a new record in pole vaulting. Unfortunately, he also set the record for The Deepest Hole Made by Someone When He Lands on the Other Side of the Bar When Another Agile Athlete Has Removed the Padding.

I chuckled. That's that, I thought. But I'd barely gotten a snicker out when Jawbreaker was back on his feet. This guy was getting on my nerves.

I grabbed a nearby football and started another play-by-play commentary: "The quarterback takes the snap. . . ."

I dropped back and motioned for the sterling scrap of stupidity to go out for the pass. It was going to be a long bomb (in more ways than one).

"It's the last play of the game. . . ."

"Go back," I shouted.

He went.

"Further back . . . back . . . !"

"Me back!" he shouted. "Me back!!"

Back he was. Straight back and over the edge of a freshly drawn cliff.

It's a pathetic sound, you know—the sound of metal connecting with the ground at 200 miles per hour. I ran to the edge of the cliff and gazed down. Yep. Jawbreaker was definitely all broken up by our little ruckus.

I thought for a minute, then made up my

ever-so-noble mind. I was going down to help put Jawbreaker back together again. I mean, if Nick could try to get along with Todd, I could do my part to "patch things up" with Jawbreaker. Besides, we cartoon types need to stick together. And who knows? When we got done putting Mr. Bucket Head back together, there just might be a couple of pieces left over that I could use in rebuilding my '63 Buick. . . .

EIGHT
Putting It All Together

McGee and Jawbreaker weren't the only ones
working out their differences; Jamie was also
working out hers. Her little crash and burn in the
snow bank yesterday had really started her to
think. So did her nonstop skate-and-fall routine
that she'd been performing all afternoon.

Now she sat on the park bench quietly unlacing
her skates. She had had enough. Ice skating was
a terrible thing—absolutely awful. Oh, sure, everyone else seemed to enjoy it. Everyone else joked
and laughed and had a great time. But for Jamie,
ice-skating was about as much fun as a date with
Freddie Kruger.

She heard some familiar voices and glanced up
to see Sarah skate by. She was gracefully weaving
in and out between her friends as they played
skate tag.

Jamie sighed. Sarah could do everything. She
could skate forward, turn corners, skate fast.
Sometimes she would even skate backwards! Then

a thought came to Jamie. She sat up and watched Sarah intently. There was something else Sarah could do.

Sarah could teach Jamie how to skate! All Jamie had to do was ask. Suddenly it seemed silly. Not asking, I mean. After all, it only made sense that instead of being jealous over Sarah's abilities Jamie could learn from them. But Jamie had wanted to do everything herself. Now, with real interesting bruises in real interesting places turning some real interesting colors, Jamie had decided to rethink this "I-can-do-it-myself!" issue.

Maybe she and Sarah could work together. Yeah. Maybe, with Sarah's help, Jamie could become a good skater. A great skater. A world renowned, triple-A, Olympic figure skater!! (Of course, right now Jamie would settle for being a skater who spent more time on her skates than on her rear.) Still, with a little practice and a lot of help, who knows how far Jamie could go?

These were the thoughts going through Jamie's mind as she watched her older sister skate . . . and these were the thoughts that were slowly helping her make up her mind.

Later that evening, after Mom made it clear that the next meal was definitely being eaten on the table, the jigsaw puzzle was about to be completed. Everyone was helping: Nick, Sarah, Jamie, Grandma, Mom, Dad. Hands were flying in all directions.

"OK, where's the other half of California?" Dad asked urgently.

"Maybe it fell into the ocean," Nick quipped.

Seeing the whole clan gathered together, Whatever came over to join in the fun. "Whatever!" Sarah complained, as she shooed the dog away. "Get your paws off the table."

He looked at her, slightly hurt at her tone of voice. It was understandable, though. There were just a few pieces left to fit in before the puzzle was done, and you could tell everyone was getting pretty excited.

"Here," Grandma said, handing Jamie a piece for the ocean. "Put that right there." But the little girl wouldn't get her fingers near the place.

"What's wrong?" Grandma asked.

"Nick says those are shark-infested waters!" she replied.

Grandma shot Nick a look as he swallowed back a snicker.

Once again, Whatever's paws were up on the table.

"Whatever! Get down . . . down!" Sarah scolded. The dog reluctantly obeyed.

"We've almost got it!" Dad was practically shouting. I guess you could say finishing a puzzle was kind of important for the big guy. "Four more pieces to go!" he repeated again and again and again. (Better make that *a lot* important.)

"Three pieces!" Mom beamed as she plopped in Oregon.

"Two," Grandma said as she slipped in the last piece for South America.

"One!" Nick grinned as he put Tasmania in place. "One more piece to go!"

The excitement was high. Soon the entire puzzle would be done . . . all 5,000 pieces. After three days of hard work, each piece would be in its perfect place. The map of the world would be complete, a testimony of the family's skill and ability to work together. It was going to be great. There was just one little problem: there were no more loose pieces on the table!

"Where did the last piece go?" Dad asked. He was starting to sound a little desperate. "It's got to be here somewhere!"

Everyone was looking. Under the puzzle, under the chairs, under the table. The kids were scrounging around on their hands and knees. So was Grandma. Things were getting serious.

"Are you sure you didn't drop it?" Mom asked Sarah. "You know when you were pushing Whatever off the . . ." Then she froze.

Everyone froze.

They slowly turned toward poor, unsuspecting Whatever. The bag of fur was over on his bed, lying as peacefully as you please, happily chowing down on . . . you guessed it . . . the last piece of puzzle!

"WHATEVER!" Everyone shouted in unison.

Now, Whatever wasn't the brightest of mutts. But by the look in everyone's eyes, he figured he just might have done something a teensy bit wrong. To double check, he gave them a little doggie smile and his best tail wag.

Uh huh, just as he suspected. No one was smiling back. He was in trouble. *Big* trouble. Maybe, just maybe, this would be a good time to take a little walk. He carefully got up, gave a casual little shake . . . then raced up the stairs for all he was worth!

"Whatever!" everyone shouted as they chased after him, "Whatever, come here, boy! Whatever. . . . here, boy!" It did no good. The more they yelled, the faster he ran. . . .

The following morning before class, Nick had a chance to talk to Todd. It's not like he really wanted to, but when you're sitting right across from each other and waiting for your teacher to arrive, which it's starting to feel like she'll never do . . . well, it's either talk to your neighbor or count all those little holes in the ceiling tile. Nick already had the number of holes memorized, so he turned to Todd.

"Hey, Todd."

The boy looked at him.

"Listen . . . ," Nicholas started, then he swallowed. This was harder than he'd figured. "I saw your poster in the library. It's really good."

The look on Todd's face showed he expected to hear just about anything *except* this. "Uh . . . thank you," he stammered.

"Really," Nick continued. "I mean, I tried drawing Jawbreaker . . . he's tough." It was funny, but talking to Todd was getting easier. In fact, Nick was almost beginning to like it. He didn't have to pretend to be better now or anything. All he had to do was be himself.

"Well, uh . . . ," Todd looked at Nicholas very carefully. Was this some sort of trick? No, Todd could see Nick was speaking from his heart. "I've, uh . . . I've had a lot of practice," he answered. Then, before he knew it, Todd was also speaking honestly. It was almost as if the sincerity from Nicholas was starting to rub off. "You know," he offered, "your stuff is really good, too."

"Thanks," Nicholas smiled. Boy, did this feel good! Maybe he should try being honest and sincere more often. "Good luck on the contest," he added.

"Thanks, Nick." Todd also was starting to feel good. "You, too."

Now, don't get me wrong. These guys weren't best of buddies. Not by a long shot. But at least they were starting to respect each other. And maybe, just maybe, a friendship would grow between them.

"Good morning, class," Mrs. Harmon said as she came whisking into the room. "We have some special news this morning! The posters for the Winter Carnival have been judged, and I'm proud to say that the winner comes from our very own classroom."

Todd and Nick fidgeted nervously in their seats. Each managed to throw a glance at the other, and each managed to give a little smile.

"The winner is . . . ," Mrs. Harmon reached for the cloth covering the poster. Then with a flourish she pulled it aside. "Derrick Cryder!"

The class gasped. Nick sat stunned. Todd's mouth fell open.

And Derrick? Derrick did what any all-American bully would do. He gloated. "Ha! I told you!" he shouted. "I told you I was better than any of you dorks! I told you!"

Nick and Todd exchanged glances once again. They weren't sure why, but suddenly both of them burst out laughing. Here they had been so sure that one of them was going to win the contest. And what happened? Derrick Cryder nailed them both!

"Couldn't happen to a worse fellow," Nick whispered over to Todd.

Todd nodded as they both continued to laugh. Neither of them knew it at the time, but their chances of becoming good friends were growing stronger by the minute.

NINE
Wrapping Up

Now, Nick's a pretty good guy. But if you ask me
(which you haven't, but I'll tell you anyway because that's my job), he's got a few too many hang-
ups for a kid. Like, he's not real keen on me eating
my world-famous dill pickle, hot pepper, and choco-
late syrup sandwiches in bed. He also has this
problem with the way I crack my toe knuckles
when I think. What really drives him crazy, though,
is when I start talking with all his friends hanging
around. He says it kinda makes them nervous
hearing voices coming from the sketch pad.

So I guess you can't blame him for slamming the
pad shut as soon as Mrs. Harmon announced the
winner. He obviously figured I had a few choice
words on the outcome. And he was right. I mean, I
know a rigged contest when I lose one.

Unfortunately, Nick didn't get around to opening
the sketch pad again until after school was out.
Now the ol' pad is a nice place to hang around, but
things can get kinda stuffy in there. Especially

when you finally find the smelly sweat socks you threw in your locker six months ago.

Then there's the boredom factor. I mean, after racquetball, a couple of hours of horseback riding, and a few laps around the pool . . . what's left?

But now we finally were able to talk. We had just arrived at the outdoor ice rink over in the park. Nick had been wanting to skate for the past few days. Now he finally felt good enough to give it a shot.

We watched as his two sisters skated past. They were working pretty well together—Sarah skating backwards and holding Jamie's outstretched arms. As for Jamie, well, she was doing great. In the next few minutes she'd definitely be skating on her own.

"So you didn't like Derrick winning the contest?" Nick asked as he finished lacing up his skates.

"You call that a contest?" I complained as I checked my pockets for my skates. (I have kinda big pockets.) Let's see, there was my tennis racket, my polo mallet, water skis. But no skates.

"Maybe it's what was best for both Todd and me."

"Right, and if you're lucky, Santa's going to leave you a good case of chicken pox in your stocking."

"No, seriously," Nick said as he eased onto his feet. He slid his skates back and forth just to get the feel of the ice. "I mean, that jealousy is pretty awful stuff . . . the way it chews at you and tries to take control. Maybe now Todd and I can start working together. Who knows, maybe we can even learn something from each other." He pushed himself off and started out on the ice. "You coming?"

"In a second," I called. I was pretty pleased with my little buddy. I mean, he makes his share of mistakes, but he always manages to learn from them. Another great trait that I'm sure he picked up from me. And he was right. He and Todd had a lot in common . . . they could learn from each other.

Kind of like me and Jawbreaker. I smiled a smugly satisfied smile. I could still see the look of gratitude on his metallic face when I'd finished putting him back together after his dive off the cliff. He had even given me a friendly pat on the back. Of course, he almost broke me in half, but I knew his heart was in the right place. (After all, I'd just put it back in a few minutes before. . . .) Yep, it felt good to know we were all learning how to get along.

Now if I could just find my skates. . . .

I checked my pockets one last time. Nope, there were definitely no skates. The closest thing I could find were a couple of large wooden matches. So with my ingenious ingenuity I hopped on, laced them to my fleet feet, and pushed off.

Things were going fine . . . for the first two and a half seconds. That was about how long it took for the friction of the ice to light the heads of the matches.

K-FOOOSH!

I disappeared faster than twenty-five cents at a video arcade. I mean, I was burning up the ice—literally. Then I ran out of ice and was just burning up. Around and around I swooshed, bouncing off one tree after another. But I wasn't worried. I'd eventually land. I'd have to. Who else was going to help Nick out on our next awesomely astounding adventure?

So stay tuned, all you snow bunnies and hockey

*pucks. Don't forget to bundle up, wear your mit-
tens, and never, never, never touch your tongue to a
frozen fire hydrant (unless you plan to stick around
until spring).*

Bye-bye, and be cool.